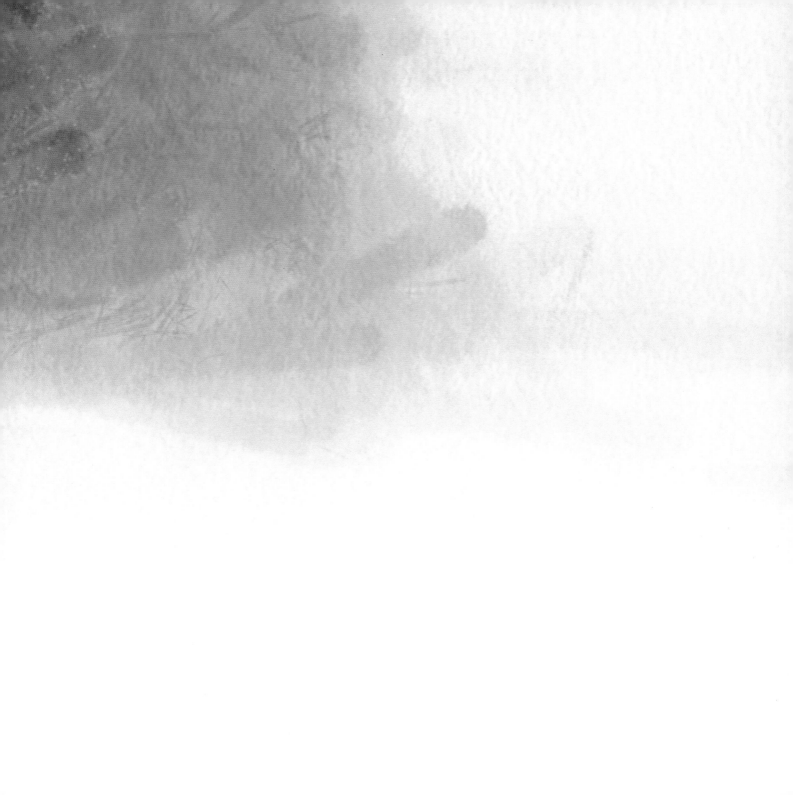

WHOSE WAR IS IT ANYWAY?

Moha Mehta

Flying Chickadee

ISBN-13:
978-0615727387 (Whose War is it Anyway?)

ISBN-10:
0615727387

First printing, January 2013
Flying Chickadee
PO Box 30021, Seattle, WA 98113-0021
www.flyingchickadee.com

Graphic Design and Illustrations ©2013 by Atelier Anonyme,
New Delhi, India.
www.anonyme.in

Dedicated to:

Children all over the world who have been displaced by the horrors of war,

and

Dr. Neera Desai
Raksha Dholakia
Narmada Dholakia
Vibhuti Dhruva
Chetana Dhru
Ro-Pri

Peace begins with a smile.

Mother Teresa

"Run!" commanded the voice inside his head. Salim leaped with catlike agility! His heart raced with fear as he dashed across town, his eyes fixed on the road. The once-peaceful town of Sanowar was quickly turning into a war zone.

Salim kept running until he reached the courtyard of his house. Catching his breath, he turned to see if anyone had followed him. An eerie silence surrounded him as he climbed the steps to the front door. "Darwaaza Kholo!" he whispered, "Open the door!"

Inside the house, Ammi was absorbed in threading a needle when she heard muffled sounds coming from the front door. Who could it be?

She glanced at her young daughter Salma, who was nursing a cold that morning. With big curious eyes, Salma watched her mother tiptoe towards the door to unlock the latch.

"Salim!" cried Ammi, surprised to see her son. Why wasn't he at school?

Salim stumbled in, heading straight for the couch. His legs wobbled with anxiety. Salma rushed to get a glass of cold water for her older brother while Ammi tried to comfort him.

Earlier that morning, he had walked across town with his best friend Asif, merrily chatting away, as they always did, on the way to school. When did their quiet little town become so dangerous?

Salim slumped into the couch.

Daadi hobbled into the front room, her wrinkled fingers linked into those of her youngest grandchild Noorie.

"What's the matter?" she asked Salim, placing her other hand on her grandson's shoulder. Her gentle manner was comforting to Salim. "Tell us what happened," she encouraged him to speak.

Noorie jumped on to Daadi's lap, ever-ready for a story. "Be gentle, little Noorie!" Ammi reminded her sprightly three-year-old.

"We were in our classroom," Salim remembered clearly. "Nawaz Sir was teaching us a lesson on the effects of—"

"Was Asif with you?" Salma interrupted her brother.

"Yes," he continued, "Asif was sitting next to me when we heard a loud BANG! The whole building shook like there was an earthquake!"

A gasp escaped Salma's lips. Noorie slipped off Daadi's lap, distracted by an ant that had wandered into the room.

"The jolt from the bang frightened us. There was a lot of commotion until Principal Zafar burst into our room ordering us to leave the school immediately. He told us that the school could be under attack."

Salim drew in a deep breath before he continued, "There wasn't any time for questions. Asif and I made a dash for the exit, bumping into students as we ran out of the building together. We ran as fast as we could without looking back until—"

Before Salim could finish his story, there were several knocks on the front door of their home. Noorie ran over to Ammi and tucked herself in her mother's lap.

Salim stood up, finding his strength. "Who's there?" he asked rather boldly. "It's me!" The voice was hushed.

"Abbu!" cried Salma recognizing the soft tones of her father's voice. Ammi raised her hands in a sign of gratitude. Daadi felt a wave of relief knowing that her son was safe.

Who's
there?

The news wasn't good. Rashid had heard that the situation in their small town was getting worse. There were sudden attacks from the air as well as fighting on the ground. Many families were planning to leave overnight. They did not feel safe enough to stay in their homes while the danger of war continued to rise.

Rashid glanced in Salim's direction as he said, "I've heard that Asif's family could be one of them." Salim felt like he was slipping into a dark hole. His mind was a tangle of confusion.

Preparations were secretly being made for those families who wished to leave Sanowar and find shelter with relatives in another town. They would be transported by trucks, which would rumble along craggy mountain roads for days before they got to a safe place.

The family was forced to make a quick decision. What should they do?

Salma's mind was whirling with questions.

What about their home? Where would they go? What would happen to their friends and relatives in Sanowar? Would they ever see them again?

Abbu tried to reason with the anxious faces staring at him all at once.

"If we stay here, Noorie will grow up in constant fear. Salim will be persuaded to join the men who are spreading this terror. We might never be able to see him again."

His voice started to weaken. "As for Salma," he said, "She can be taken away from us, and her dream to study hard and become something will be crushed."

Ammi and Daadi shared an unspoken message. Things were going to change very fast for their family!

Noorie snuggled up to Daadi, unable to understand why nobody had a smile to share with her today.

"Abbu," said Salim, "No matter how much we love Sanowar, the danger of living here is growing every day." He sounded like a grown-up, way beyond his twelve young years!

Salma nodded in agreement with her brother. "The war will destroy everything good in Sanowar," she said, wearing a solemn expression.

It was getting dark. The waning moon w
The only sound outside was that of a str
The decision was final. Before the first lig
following morning, Rashid's family woul
Sanowar.

"What should we pack?" asked Salma, fe
scared at the same time. "A few clothes,"
"What about Daadi?" Ammi wanted to k
go with us," Abbu was brisk. "When will
home again?" The question popped out
don't know," Abbu replied. "I have to ma
arrangements."

He left abruptly.

"Be careful!" Ammi warned her husband

It was past everyone's bedtime when Abbu returned. He had barely put his head to the pillow when there was a knock on the door. Noorie rubbed her sleepy little eyes. Who was at the door?

The tall man at the door was a volunteer. His face was covered with a scarf. He was one of the many good men who helped families escape the terrors of war.

He was there to assist Salim's family to a waiting truck. The truck would carry them to another town where Rashid's family would have to begin anew. The time had come to walk away from all that they had known and loved.

"Where are we going?" whispered Daadi as she wobbled along the road with the help of a walking stick.

"Somewhere safe, mama jaan," Rashid addressed his mother affectionately. Ammi stayed close to Daadi as they kept moving in the direction of the truck.

"Why are we whispering?" Salma mumbled, adjusting Noorie's weight in her arms.

Abbu tried to hide the fear in his voice. "We don't want to be caught by the men who carry hate in their hearts," he replied in a low voice. "C'mon Salim!" he egged on his trailing son.

Rashid's family walked as fast as they could. It was still dark outside. As they got closer, the truck looked like a giant shadow.

One by one, they clambered on. Daadi was the first to be helped. Ammi was next. Abbu held Noorie while Salma jumped on to the truck. While she was climbing, she noticed a figure at the far end. "Asif!" She let out a cry of delight. "Shhh!" cautioned Salim, turning his head sharply.

Seeing Asif crouched in the corner was enough to bring a smile to his face. He jumped on to the truck and squeezed into the small space next to his best friend.

"Hurry!" The truck driver's command was hushed. "We must get out of here before day breaks."

Abbu and Noorie were the last ones to board the truck. There was a rumble as the engine started. They were off! A cloud of dust emerged as the truck, filled with families who did not know where they were headed, crawled out of Sanowar. All they wished for was a life without fear.

Very soon, chirping birds would announce the arrival of a new day in Sanowar. Rashid narrowed his gaze. The town so dear to them was disappearing into the horizon.

We will be back some day…We will!

The morning light slowly spread hope as the truck bounced along the dusty road.